For William Ezra Ziefert
—H. M. Z.

For Isak
—D. S.

Atheneum Books for Young Readers
An imprint of Simon & Schuster Children's Publishing Division
1230 Avenue of the Americas
New York, New York 10020

Book design by Michael Nelson
The text of this book is set in Stempel Schneidler.
The illustrations are rendered in gouache.

First Edition
Printed in China for Harriet Ziefert, Inc.
10 9 8 7 6 5 4 3 2 1

Library of Congress Cataloging-in-Publication Data
Ziefert, Harriet M.
Wee G. / by Harriet M. Ziefert ; illustrated by Donald Saaf.—1st ed.
p. cm.
"An Anne Schwartz book."
Summary: A kitten spends an eventful day chasing butterflies,
rolling in the dirt, and getting lost and then finding her way back home.
ISBN 0-689-81064-4
[1. Cats—Fiction.] I. Saaf, Donald, ill. II. Title.
PZ7.Z487We   1997
[E]—dc20
96-4203

Wee G.

written by Harriet M. Ziefert

illustrated by Donald Saaf

An Anne Schwartz Book

Atheneum Books for Young Readers

This is Wee G.

Early every morning she jumps out of bed,

takes a quick drink of milk and . . .

. . . runs out to play.

Wee G. knows just what she wants to do.

"Today I will roll in the dirt," says Wee G.

"Then I will sit quietly and wait for a friend."

Something is buzzing around Wee G.
"Go away, bee!" she says.
"You're bothering me."

Something else is flying by.
Not a bee. A butterfly!
"Butterfly, will you play with me?" she asks.

"Please play with me!

I know a good game.

Hey, come back!"

Uh-oh, where is Wee G.?
She can't find the butterfly.

And she can't find her way.
"I don't want to be lost!" she cries.

Wee G. tries to be brave.
She looks high . . .

. . . and low.

"Hello, ladybug," says Wee G.

"Do you know the way to my house?"

The ladybug does not know.

Wee G. wanders and wanders until she comes to a path.

She sees pawprints . . .

a fence . . .

a garden . . .

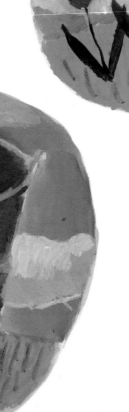

a bucket!

"I'm not lost!" says Wee G.

"You're home, my brave Wee G.," says her mother.

"And you're just in time for supper."

"I was scared," says Wee G.

"But now I'm happy."

Good night, Wee G.